THE OLDEST SWIMMER IN TOWN

Old Buttspry Primary School

OB PS

Name: Mabel Agnes Gladstone Muttley

Class: 5

Teacher: Mr Dibble

English	Written - Mabel would make better progress if she could be persuaded to use pen and paper instead of her slate. Spoken - Mabel is never at a loss for words. Unfortunately.
Maths	Mabel usually finishes the Numeracy Hour in ten minutes and spends the rest of the time polishing her abacus and tidying out her handbag.
History	Mabel has a vast knowledge of twentieth century history, but must get out of the habit of writing as if she was there at the time.
Drama	Mabel enjoys these sessions and makes imaginative use of her handbag.
Music	Since Mabel's first class singing lesson, when we all spent half an hour looking for a wounded cat, Mabel has been put in charge of the maracas.
Design Technology	All Mabel's work has been made with items she keeps in her handbag. Her scale model of Buckingham Palace made using hair curlers, corn plasters and an old corset has been much admired.
PE	Mabel is very sprightly and shows a lot of enthusiasm. However, she would do better if she put down her handbag.
General comments	Mabel has settled in quickly to Old Buttspry Primary and is a very popular member of the school. She obviously feels at home, as she wears her bedroom slippers in the classroom. Although Mabel shows a degree of independence well beyond her years, I am concerned about her need to cling to her handbag.
Head Teacher's comments	Well done, Mabel. Targets for next term - try not to take over Mr Dibble's history lessons. Remember that staff cannot be expected to come round at playtime with tea and biscuits. Try not to refer to members of staff as 'young so and so'.

Head of School .... *Ribble* ....

Class Teacher .... *Bleat* ....

Days late   0

Days absent 0

THE OLDEST SWIMMER IN TOWN

BURCHETT & VOGLER

Illustrated by
Tim Archbold

BLOOMSBURY
CHILDREN'S
BOOKS

For Audrey Burchett, with love

First published in Great Britain in 1999
Bloomsbury Publishing Plc, 38 Soho Square, London, W1V 5DF

The moral right of the author has been asserted
A CIP catalogue record of this book is available from the
British Library

ISBN 0 7475 4260 0

Printed in England by Clays Ltd, St Ives plc

10 9 8 7 6 5 4 3 2 1

One

One Friday morning a big poster appeared on the Old Buttspry Primary School notice-board.

Children were jostling each other to sign up.

'We've never had a gala before!'

'My turn now.'

'I hope I win a ribbon.'

Finally there were only two pupils left. Jodie Bunn looked at the list.

'Got a pen, Mabel?' she asked her friend. 'I'm going to put my name down.'

Mabel Muttley delved into a large black handbag that was hanging on her arm and produced an old-fashioned fountain pen.

'Here you are, dearie,' she said. She peered at the poster through her glasses. 'Hmmm . . . let me see now. Put me down for every race.'

Jodie stared at her skinny friend with the great, long flat feet and baggy school uniform.

'You're amazing, Mabel,' she gasped. 'I know you're very fit, but won't you be exhausted after swimming every race?' She looked round to make sure there was

no one to overhear. 'Don't forget you're a hundred and nine,' she whispered.

'A hundred and ten in August!' said Mabel proudly.

No one else at the school knew Mabel Muttley's real age. A hundred years ago, when she was nine, she'd had to leave Old Buttspry Primary to go to work as a servant. And now she'd come back to finish her education where she'd left off. Her teacher, Mr Dibble, and the head, Miss

Bleat, had no idea that Mabel had been born a century before the rest of class five. When she'd presented her birth certificate to them she'd accidentally had her thumb over the year of her birth. As far as they were concerned, she was just an unusual looking nine-year-old who'd probably sat in the bath for too long.

At that moment, Mabel heard soft, sneaking footsteps coming up behind her.

She spun round. There stood the nastiest boy in the class – sly and shifty Sidney Scrimshanks.

'Hello, Sidney,' said Mabel. 'Come to sign up for the swimming competition?'

'I'm not bothering with that rubbish,' scoffed Sidney, with a sneer. 'Got better things to do.'

'Like pinching, kicking and hiding people's books?' muttered Jodie.

'Oh go on, Sidney,' cackled Mabel. 'There's nothing like a spot of exercise, as Grandma Muttley said when she set off to climb Mount Everest on her eighty-sixth birthday.'

'I'm not going to a stupid gala,' shouted Sidney, 'just to see you lot having fun!'

'You haven't got much choice,' laughed Jodie. 'It says on the poster that the whole school's going.'

Sidney's face screwed into an evil grimace.

'I'm telling my dad,' he whined.

They all jumped as a deep voice suddenly boomed down the corridor.

'Who's been upsetting my little Sidney?'

Two

Sidney's dad marched pompously down the corridor towards them.

Councillor Cedric Scrimshanks was always popping up at Old Buttspry Primary. He was a school governor and considered himself to be in charge. So did everyone else – even the caretaker, who swept his parking space carefully every morning. Although since Mabel had arrived at the school, Councillor Scrimshanks found that somehow he didn't always get his own way any more.

Sidney's dad stopped to check his reflection in the glass of a classroom door, adjusted the creases in his suit, straightened his tie and strode up to his son.

'What's going on?' he demanded.

Mabel stuck out her hand.

'Nice to see you, sir,' she cackled, pumping his arm up and down enthusiastically.

'Oh, it's you,' said Councillor Scrimshanks, snatching back his hand as quickly as he could. He eyed Mabel as if she was a rattlesnake. 'What have you been doing to my Sidney?'

'Dad!' whined Sidney, grabbing his arm. 'It's not fair, Dad. There's going to be a

gala and I can't enter and I won't win anything and everyone else will be having fun!'

'Nonsense, son,' said his dad firmly. 'You're a Scrimshanks. You can beat anyone you want to.'

'No I can't!' hissed Sidney.

He reached up and whispered something in his father's ear. Councillor Scrimshanks's eyes narrowed and he read the poster carefully.

'My Sidney not win anything?' he growled. 'We'll see about that!'

He marched Sidney off towards Miss Bleat's office.

'They're all the same, those Scrimshankses,' cackled Mabel when they'd gone. 'Always wanting to be top dog. I remember when I was at this school a hundred years ago. Sidney's great-great-grandfather had a tantrum when teacher disqualified him from the three-legged race after he ran it on his roller-skates.'

'I wonder what Councillor Scrimshanks has got planned this time,' said Jodie. 'It's bound to be something devious to make Sidney come out the winner.'

'In that case, you and I had better keep an eye on them,' cackled Mabel. 'Now there's just one little thing I've got to do before the gala.'

'What's that?' asked Jodie.

'Learn to swim, dearie.'

Three

On Monday morning Mabel walked briskly along the corridor towards her classroom. Jodie dragged along behind. They had spent the whole weekend at the leisure centre trying to teach Mabel to swim. Jodie was rather tired. She'd had to do a lot of lifesaving.

'Roll on Thursday!' declared Mabel as she sat down at her table in the classroom, pulled a pair of bedroom slippers out of her handbag and put them on. 'I can't wait for the gala – now that I can swim.'

'Are you sure you're quite ready?' asked Jodie, wearily plonking herself down in the seat opposite. 'The only race you'll win at the moment is the race to the bottom of the pool.'

'Mind your tongue, girl! retorted Mabel. 'A couple more lessons and I'll be fine. And anyway, it's not the winning, it's the taking part, as Grandma Muttley said

when she ran the marathon at ninety-three.'

Sidney sidled over and took his place next to Mabel. He had his usual evil look on his face as he began to rummage in his pocket. Mabel gave him a cheery smile.

'Looking for this?' she cackled, handing him back a rather vicious looking mouse-trap.

'I'm going to get you!' snarled Sidney. 'I know it was you that stuck that notice on my back last Friday.'

'What notice, Sidney?' asked Mabel brightly.

'The one with "Kick me!" on it,' hissed Sidney. 'It was meant for you! I mean . . .'

'Oh, that notice!' chortled Mabel. 'I recognised your writing and thought you might want it back.'

'Just you wait, Mabel Muttley!' growled Sidney. 'I'm going to . . .'

Mr Dibble, their teacher, came bumbling into the classroom reading a piece of paper.

'I've got a message from Miss Bleat,' he exclaimed. 'It's about the gala.'

Jodie looked suspiciously at Sidney. Sidney was leaning back in his chair. A smug expression was creeping over his weaselly face.

'Important notice!' read Mr Dibble. Class five went silent. 'Our esteemed school governor, Councillor Scrimshanks, has quite rightly pointed out that the gala is unfair to those who cannot swim. Therefore the school swimming gala will not go ahead as planned.'

Four

A groan of disappointment went around the classroom. Class five had been talking of nothing else since they'd seen the notice for the gala. Only Jodie perked up. At least she wouldn't have to give Mabel any more swimming lessons.

'Excuse me, sir, but that's outrageous!' piped up Mabel. She waved her handbag angrily. 'Cancelling the competition, I mean. I'm not going to take that lying down. I'm going to chain myself to the railings in protest. It wouldn't be the first time either.'

'I don't think you need to do that, Mabel,' said Mr Dibble anxiously. 'The school swimming gala will not go ahead as

originally planned because an extra race has been added!'

Sighs of relief went round the class. Jodie put her head in her hands.

'Indeed, it will be the most important race in the gala,' Mr Dibble went on, 'and the winner will receive the Cedric Scrimshanks Cup.'

Mabel stuck up her hand.

'Excuse me, sir,' she said politely, 'but what's that when it's at home?'

'It's a magnificent golden cup!' exclaimed Mr Dibble enthusiastically. 'Kindly donated by Sidney's father. I polished it for him myself this morning!'

'I bet it's already got Sidney's name engraved on it!' muttered Jodie.

'Here are the rules,' read Mr Dibble. 'Number one – Anyone at school can enter, even teachers. Number two – No engines. Number three – Boats must be home-made.' There was a buzz of excited conversation as everyone started talking

about the sort of boat they were going to build. Mr Dibble scratched his head thoughtfully. 'Not much time to construct a craft for Thursday,' he muttered to himself. 'Wait a minute. I've got an old blackboard somewhere . . . and those inflatable globes would come in handy . . .' He suddenly realised where he was. 'What's all this chatting, class five? Get out your English books and finish your poems about Fergus the Thermos Flask . . .'

Mr Dibble disappeared into his stockroom.

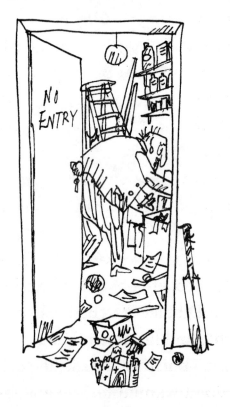

'I don't know why he's bothering to build a boat,' sneered Sidney loudly as the class got out their exercise books. 'I'm entering the race and my craft will be unbeatable. No one else stands a chance.'

Everyone's face fell. If Sidney was entering the race the rest of them might just as well forget it. The Scrimshankses always made sure they won.

Mabel gave Sidney a suspicious look. Then she rummaged in her handbag and produced her slate and pencil.

'Can't wait till Thursday!' she said to Jodie.

The nearby children stuffed their fingers in their ears as she scratched loudly away at her poem.

Jodie took a deep breath and leaned across the table to her. She couldn't put it off any longer. She had to tell her friend the truth about her swimming.

'Erm . . . your lesson tonight, Mabel,' she said. 'I don't want to disappoint you but I think we'd better cancel it . . . After all, you keep sinking and . . . well, let's face it, Mabel. You'll never be a swimmer.'

Mabel looked up.

'What was that, dearie?' she asked innocently. 'I was busy with me poem. Can you give us a rhyme for cocoa?'

Jodie shook her head.

'And by the way,' Mabel went on. 'I don't want to disappoint you, seeing as how you've enjoyed our lessons so much, but I'm going to pull out of the swimming races – to give the others a chance.'

'So you won't be going in for the gala after all!' exclaimed Jodie in relief.

'Oh yes I will, dearie!' declared Mabel. 'You see, me elbows are itching.'

Jodie sat to attention. Mabel's elbows itched whenever there was trickery afoot. Mabel held her slate up so that Sidney couldn't hear.

'I reckon Sidney and his dad have got a sneaky plan worked out,' she whispered, 'so Sidney does win that cup. I've never known a Scrimshanks to win anything without cheating.'

'What can we do about it?' Jodie whispered back.

'I'm going to bring that Sidney down a peg or two,' cackled Mabel. 'However much he cheats, I'll make sure he doesn't win the race.'

'How are you going to do that?' asked Jodie.

'Easy as pie, dearie,' said Mabel. 'I'm going to build meself a boat.'

Five

At lunchtime next day the sound of banging could be heard all over the school. It was coming from the direction of the head's office. Miss Bleat had kindly allowed the competitors to use her room to make their boats.

Mabel was hard at work hammering the sides of an old tin bath. Jodie was frowning at a long list in her hand.

'Listen, Mabel!' she shouted above the din. 'I've managed to get the broom, the old bike, the sink plunger and the three-legged stool, but I'll never find butter churners!'

Mabel put down her hammer and peered at Jodie over her glasses.

'Nonsense, girl!' she said briskly. 'Don't give up so easily, as Grandma Muttley told that nice Mr Carter when he couldn't find the door to Tutankhamun's pyramid. Now, pass me that tin-opener.'

The head tottered past on her way to dinner. She was wearing fluffy earmuffs to drown out the noise.

'How's it going, Mabel my dear?' she asked weakly.

'First rate, Miss Bleat!' shouted Mabel. 'Never had so much fun in all me life!'

'Ah, the enthusiasm of the young!' twittered Miss Bleat, giving her pupil a feeble pat on the head.

'There's one thing I don't understand, Mabel,' said Jodie, when Miss Bleat had gone. 'If Sidney's so keen to win the boat race, why isn't he here making a boat?'

Mabel nodded over towards Miss Bleat's stockroom. There was a chair placed in front of the door, and seated on it was a huge man in a chauffeur's uniform. It was

Councillor Scrimshanks's latest driver, Big Bert. Big Bert had his arms folded and he looked mean.

'I reckon Sidney's got something going on in there,' whispered Mabel. 'Me elbows are itching something shocking!'

'We need to check it out,' said Jodie. 'But we'll never get past Big Bert.'

'Won't we?' cackled Mabel. 'Excuse me, young man,' she called politely to the driver. 'You look hungry. I expect you'd like one of my sandwiches.'

The driver glared suspiciously at her. Jodie stared. What on earth was Mabel doing?

'Councillor Scrimshanks says I mustn't leave my chair,' said the surly driver, but he licked his lips at the thought of some lunch.

Mabel opened her handbag and peered in. 'I've got tuna and pickle, onion and cucumber, sausage and mango chutney, and loads more . . . why don't you come and choose?'

The driver glanced shiftily round, then he got up and lumbered over to Mabel and her handbag.

'Quick!' whispered Mabel to Jodie. 'Have a peep while he's busy.'

As soon as the driver was busy sorting through Mabel's sandwich selection, Jodie crept up to the door and peered through the keyhole.

In the middle of Miss Bleat's large stockroom an extraordinary sight met her eye. Sidney Scrimshanks sat in the corner reading a comic, his feet up on a shelf. A man in a white coat was studying some complicated plans, and two others were bent over something that Jodie couldn't quite see.

Then one of the men moved back and Jodie gave a gasp of horror as she caught a glimpse of what they were working on. At that moment, Big Bert, munching a cheese and sprout sandwich, turned and saw her.

''Ere,' he shouted. 'What are you up to?'

'She's just keeping your chair warm,' explained Mabel.

'That's okay then,' said Big Bert. 'As long as you weren't looking through the keyhole.'

'That was a close shave,' hissed Jodie as she scampered back to Mabel. 'You were right. Sidney is up to something! And from what I've seen you don't stand a chance on Thursday, Mabel!'

Six

It was Thursday afternoon and the whole of Old Buttspry Primary were at the leisure centre. Children in damp swimming costumes milled about showing off their winners' ribbons, and the spectators' gallery was crammed with pupils and their families. Miss Bleat and Councillor Scrimshanks sat at a table by the side of the pool. The Cedric Scrimshanks Cup sat gleaming in front of them. Everyone was waiting for the final event of the school gala – the boat race.

Mabel and Jodie were down on the tiled beach where all the boats were lined up ready for the race. They were putting the final touches to the Muttley Marine Craft.

'Hoist the mainsail, me old shipmate!' ordered Mabel.

'Aye, aye, Cap'n,' answered Jodie as she tied Mabel's lucky hankies to the mast.

'I was pleased as punch when you won the backstroke,' said Mabel, giving her bath a final polish.

'I thought my mum was going to fall out of the gallery cheering,' laughed Jodie, looking proudly at the red ribbon pinned to her costume. 'Pity your mother couldn't be here, Mabel.'

'Yes,' sighed Mabel sadly. 'But of course it's impossible. She always goes to karate on a Thursday afternoon.'

Jodie looked over at Sidney who was sauntering up and down the beach, sneering loudly at the other competitors' home-made craft. His own boat was covered by a tarpaulin and Big Bert was standing guard over it.

'And now for the final touch,' cackled Mabel. She pulled a stripy sailors' jumper out of her handbag and put it on over her baggy school skirt. 'I haven't worn this since the time I tried to run away to sea!'

'Listen, Mabel,' Jodie whispered, 'are you sure you want to go in for this race? You haven't seen Sidney's boat yet. It's . . .'

'I've told you,' said Mabel firmly. 'I don't want to hear about Sidney's boat. Whatever it's like, it can't be as good as mine.'

'But Mabel,' insisted Jodie. 'Yours is only a tin bath.'

'Wash your mouth out, girl!' snapped Mabel. 'You can't go on appearances, as Grandma Muttley said when she bet all her savings on the three-legged dog at the greyhound races. The Muttley Marine Craft won't let us down!'

A feeble cough came over the loud speaker. 'And now,' quavered Miss Bleat's voice, 'we come to the final event. As you know, this is the most important race of the gala, and is taking place thanks to Councillor Scrimshanks.' Sidney's dad

stood up and bowed. One or two people clapped. 'The competitors must go once round the leisure pool,' continued Miss Bleat, 'and the winner will receive the Cedric Scrimshanks Gold Cup.'

The leisure pool was huge. The competitors were going to have to cross the pool, race round the lazy river, paddle past the fountain and steer behind the waterfall. The first one to complete the course and reach the bridge by the Jacuzzi would be the winner.

'And remember,' added Miss Bleat, 'all non-swimmers must wear a rubber ring.'

'I won't be using one of those!' declared Sidney loudly as he strutted over to his tarpaulin covered boat. 'I'm an excellent swimmer!'

'If he's so good, why didn't he enter any of the swimming races,' muttered Jodie. She looked anxiously at her friend. 'You'll need one, won't you, Mabel.'

'Don't be silly, dearie,' cackled her

wrinkly friend. 'After all those lessons you gave me?'

She took up her position beside the Muttley Marine Craft, handbag over her arm.

Mr Dibble was next to her. He had fitted four inflatable globes underneath a blackboard and was carrying an extra long ruler to use as a punting pole.

On his left was Cynthia Smith from class six. She'd made a scale model of the Cutty Sark, correct in every detail down to the pig pen and the bilge pump.

Harry and Barry, the Twittington twins from class four, had identical lilos with hippopotamus heads glued on the front.

Mrs Sweep, the caretaker, stood next to her converted wheelbarrow clutching two spades for oars. Tiddles her cat sat by her side, wearing an armband. And last in the line was Charlie Tucker, the cook, who had brought along an enormous saucepan and a ladle.

Mabel stood proudly by her bath. It had a broom as a mast with Mabel's lucky hankies tied as pennants. Two butter churners were fixed to the side and turned by bicycle pedals.

'Good luck, Mabel,' said Jodie.

'She'll need it!' smirked Sidney. 'Unveil the SS Victory, Big Bert.'

Big Bert pulled the tarpaulin off Sidney's boat with a flourish.

A gasp of amazement went round the leisure centre.

Seven

The SS Victory stood gleaming in the bright lights of the leisure centre. It was long, streamlined and bright red. It had a windscreen, a padded seat and a leather covered steering wheel. There was a metal figurehead at the front, in the shape of a

shark. Sidney's craft looked like a fast, expensive speedboat.

Jodie turned to Mabel. 'Sidney was right. His boat is unbeatable. He'll be past the finishing line before the rest of you have started.'

'Don't give up, girl,' retorted Mabel. 'It's not over till it's over, as Grandma Muttley said when her horse fell at the first fence in the Grand National and she had to carry it the rest of the way.'

She began to whistle happily as she pushed her boat into the water.

The spectators were grumbling and pointing at the SS Victory.

'No one else stands a chance!'

'Sidney Scrimshanks never made that!'

'That's cheating, that is!'

Miss Bleat looked nervous. Councillor Scrimshanks patted her on the hand.

'Of course it's all his own work,' he said soothingly. 'Such a talented boy. Takes after his father.'

'Oh well, in that case, I'm sure it will be all right,' said Miss Bleat in relief. 'Everyone in their boats please.'

Mabel hopped into her Muttley Marine Craft, pulled a Primus stove, kettle and tea set out of her handbag and arranged them neatly at her feet.

With great ceremony, Big Bert slid the SS Victory into the water. Sidney swaggered over and leapt in. He settled himself on his plush seat, checked his rear-view mirror and flicked a switch on the dashboard. There was a quiet mechanical humming and a suspicious bubbling of water coming from under his boat.

'Oh dear,' quavered Miss Bleat. 'I don't think engines are allowed . . .'

'That's no engine,' said Councillor Scrimshanks smoothly. 'It's just the aerodynamic alignment of the keel flanges.'

'Oh . . . jolly good,' gulped the head.

Jodie was watching Sidney closely. She was surprised to see that on the seat next to him was a notebook with a list of the competitors written on it.

'Boats ready?' called Miss Bleat into the microphone. 'Contenders ready?'

She blew her whistle and the boat race began.

Eight

The first ever Old Buttspry Primary School Boat Race was underway. The spectators in the viewing gallery let out a great cheer for the brave competitors. No one cheered for Sidney.

'Anchors aweigh!' cackled Mabel. She set her kettle to boil on the stove, turned her pedals happily and sped after the others towards the lazy river.

When her kettle started to whistle, Mabel made herself a pot of tea and then checked round for Sidney.

Two competitors were still at the starting post. One was Charlie the cook, who hadn't got the hang of rowing a saucepan and was going round in circles, creating a

small whirlpool. The other was Sidney Scrimshanks. The SS Victory hadn't moved. Mabel chuckled to herself and pedalled along the lazy river, steaming past the Cutty Sark.

Back at the beach, the SS Victory suddenly roared into life. It ploughed along the leisure pool, sending water crashing against the sides, and swept into the lazy river. There was a gasp from the

spectators as it headed after Mrs Sweep
and Tiddles who were bringing up the
rear. Sidney zoomed past the wheelbarrow,
swamping it with a huge wave. The
wheelbarrow promptly sank with a glug.

From her position at the starting post,

Jodie saw Sidney snigger and cross a name off his list. She realised with horror what he was planning. To make sure he won, Sidney Scrimshanks was going to sink everybody else. Jodie had to warn Mabel. She knew that no one was allowed on the side of the pool while the race was going on, but this was serious. Mabel could be in danger. Making sure no one was looking, she began to edge her way around the leisure pool.

The crowd hadn't noticed Sidney. They were too busy yelling for the leaders – Mr Dibble and Mabel. The blackboard and the bath tub were neck and neck as they pulled out of the lazy river. But as Mabel pedalled into the lead, she started to twitch and wriggle in her seat. Her elbows had begun to itch.

The Twittington twins were bringing up the rear. Sidney zoomed up behind them. He leaned over the side of his boat, sneakily pulled the stopper out of Harry

Twittington's lilo and crossed another name off his list. Then he roared along towards the second lilo.

'Go on, my son!' yelled Councillor Scrimshanks.

Sidney gave his dad a triumphant wave and turned back to deal with Barry Twittington. To his horror, he found Mabel and her tin bath right in front of him. Sidney let out a shriek and in his panic pulled the steering wheel round too hard.

He missed the Muttley Marine Craft by millimetres and hit the side of the pool. The metal shark on the front of his boat wedged itself in a grille. The SS Victory was stuck.

'Dad!' he yelled, frantically flicking switches on the dashboard. 'Get me out!'

'Sorry, Sidney,' cackled Mabel. 'I just popped back to make sure you were still afloat.' She waved her teapot at him. 'Fancy a cuppa?'

Sidney looked as if he was going to explode.

'Perhaps another time then,' said Mabel. 'Full steam ahead!'

She set off, pedalling furiously, to catch up with the race.

Councillor Scrimshanks strode round the side of the pool.

'Don't worry, son,' he said. 'I'll soon have you out of there.'

He clicked his fingers and Big Bert lumbered over and started to struggle with the shark.

'But I'm last!' shouted Sidney, stamping his feet on the bottom of his boat. 'And they're all ahead of me, and that stupid Mabel Muttley in her stupid bath tried to drown me and I'm going to lose!'

'You'd better not,' said Councillor Scrimshanks. 'I've already had your name engraved on the cup. Don't worry about Mabel Muttley, Sidney – or the others.' He looked round furtively. 'You're forgetting the Scrimshanks Scuttler.'

A smug smirk slowly spread itself over Sidney's face. He reached down between his feet and pulled out something sharp and shiny.

Nine

'The Secret Scrimshanks Scuttler won't let you down,' whispered Sidney's dad, as Big Bert finally freed the SS Victory. 'It'll drill a hole in anything – and no one will suspect a thing.'

Sidney slipped the Scuttler into the water, picked up a small remote control device and pushed its lever forwards.

Meanwhile Jodie was crawling round the pool, keeping hidden behind the plastic plants. She crouched beside the waterfall and waited for the boats to arrive. It wasn't long before the leaders came into view.

Mabel was in the lead, heading past the octopus fountain with Mr Dibble, Barry Twittington and Cynthia Smith close behind. There was no sign of the SS Victory.

'Mabel!' hissed Jodie. 'Keep a lookout for Sidney! He must be lurking somewhere. He's out to sink all the boats in the race!'

Mabel pulled a telescope out of her handbag and scanned the horizon. 'I see no Scrimshankses!' she cackled. 'Don't worry, dearie. Last time I spied him he was marooned.'

She pedalled on purposefully, butter churners ploughing through the water.

Jodie looked anxiously back down the course. She gasped as she saw something fast and silvery speeding along under the water. Strange things began to happen. There was a flash of silver under Barry Twittington's lilo and the lilo instantly disappeared beneath him. One of the globes supporting Mr Dibble's blackboard burst with a loud pop and class five's teacher slid into the water still clutching his ruler. And all that could be seen of the

Cutty Sark was the flag on the mast
flapping feebly above the surface.

'Do you think we should stop the race,
Councillor Scrimshanks?' quavered Miss
Bleat.

'Of course not,' said Mr Scrimshanks
firmly as a dripping Mr Dibble mooched
past towards the changing room. 'Not our
fault if they didn't make their boats
properly.'

Sidney roared up to the octopus
fountain, and gleefully crossed three more

names off his list. Then he saw Mabel ahead of him, pedalling cheerfully towards the waterfall. The spectators knew who they wanted to win.

'Mabel!' they cheered. 'Come on, Mabel!'

'Look out, Mabel!' shouted Jodie, leaning forward and nearly falling in the water.

With an evil grin on his weaselly face, Sidney picked up his remote control. The Secret Scrimshanks Scuttler went shooting across the water, vicious corkscrew whirling.

'Bless my bloomers!' exclaimed Mabel as the silver torpedo headed straight for her boat.

There was a muffled clang and the Scuttler cannoned into the side of Mabel's bath tub. The tin boat shuddered violently in the water and rocked from side to side. The hankies on the mast flapped wildly. The Muttley Marine Craft disappeared through the cascading curtain of the waterfall.

Ten

Sidney began to snigger. He licked the end of his pencil and, with a flourish, crossed Mabel's name off his list. Then he grasped the steering wheel and prepared to cross the finishing line in style. The Cedric Scrimshanks Gold Cup was his!

Suddenly he heard a strange whine, like a wounded wasp. It was the Scuttler. It whizzed round in drunken circles, broke into strange zigzags and lurched straight towards him!

'Dad!' shrieked Sidney. 'It's going to get me!' He tugged and twisted the lever on his handset. But the Scuttler continued on its collision course. Sidney leapt on to his seat and screamed.

'What can be the matter?' asked Miss Bleat.

'No idea,' muttered Councillor Scrimshanks, nervously fiddling with his tie. 'Perhaps he's seasick.'

A gush of water shot up like a whale's spout as the Scuttler hit the SS Victory amidships. Sidney's boat sank like a stone taking Sidney with it.

'Help!' he yelled as he surfaced, flapping his arms wildly. 'I can't swim!'

'Somebody save my boy!' yelled Councillor Scrimshanks.

'Right-o, sir,' came a cheery voice. 'Won't be a sec.'

The Muttley Marine Craft appeared from behind the waterfall. A slightly damp Mabel was pedalling along, bailing out water with her teapot.

'You're all right, Mabel!' gasped Jodie.

'Right as a trivet!' declared her wrinkly friend. She tapped the side of her bath. 'This is unsinkable. Nothing like a solid bit of tin, as Grandma Muttley said when she whacked a burglar over the head with her baking tray.'

Mabel flung off her school skirt. Standing in her big red bloomers she held her nose and jumped into the water, handbag over her arm.

'Mabel!' shrieked Jodie. 'You don't know how to . . .'

She stopped. Mabel was swimming! It was a very odd stroke. Her right elbow

was sticking up like a shark's fin with her
handbag hooked over it and her left arm
was spinning wildly. Her legs were doing
doggy paddle as she moved swiftly
towards the floundering Sidney. As soon
as he saw her Sidney reached out and
grabbed her tightly round the neck. They
both disappeared under the surface. The
spectators gasped in horror. All that could
be seen was Mabel's handbag, bobbing
forlornly on the water.

Eleven

For a moment there was stunned silence around the leisure centre. Then, all of a sudden, Mabel popped up from under the water. She was clutching Sidney by the scruff of his neck. With a deft flick, she draped him over her handbag and towed him to the side of the pool.

Jodie ran over.

'How did you manage to save him?' she gasped as she helped Mabel haul him out. 'And what have you done to him?' Sidney lay on the tiles, staring at the ceiling, with a stupid grin on his face.

'Simple, dearie,' cackled Mabel, clinging to the side of the pool. 'I used the Muttley Hypnotising Manoeuvre.

Always came in useful when I worked at the zoo.'

'You're amazing, Mabel!' said Jodie. 'Give us your hand. I'll help you out.'

'Don't be silly, dearie,' said Mabel. She turned and began to splash back to her boat, clutching her handbag. 'I've got a race to finish!'

She clambered into her bath, wrung out her bloomers and started pedalling. Cheered on by the spectators, she made for the finishing line. As she passed the Jacuzzi and sailed under the bridge, a great cheer went up from the crowd.

'Well done, Mabel!'

'What a hero!'

'Mabel's won the cup!'

Councillor Scrimshanks stood up, took the microphone and strutted importantly over to where Sidney lay on the poolside. He clicked his fingers. Big Bert lumbered over and tucked Sidney under his arm.

'It's only fair to my brave little son . . . er, I mean, to all the gallant competitors,' announced Councillor Scrimshanks, 'that I declare the winner of the boat race to be . . . nobody.'

There was angry muttering from the gallery. Councillor Scrimshanks ignored it.

Then someone tapped him on the arm. He turned round to find Mabel and Jodie standing beside him.

'Excuse me, sir,' said Mabel politely, 'but I believe this is yours.'

She delved into her handbag and pulled out the battered remains of the Scrimshanks Scuttler.

'Shall we show it to Miss Bleat?' said Jodie helpfully.

Councillor Scrimshanks turned bright red, snatched the Scuttler and stuffed it under his jacket.

'As I was saying,' he growled into the microphone, 'I declare the winner of the boat race to be nobody . . . other than Mabel Muttley!' He turned to Big Bert.

'Phone the engravers,' he snarled. 'We've got to change the name on the cup.'

Mabel shook Councillor Scrimshanks delightedly by the hand. Then she swept the Cedric Scrimshanks Gold Cup off the table and held it high above her head. The crowd went wild.